My 1st Classic Story

Beauty
and the
Beast

a retelling by Christianne C. Jones

illustrated by Amy Bailey Muehlenhardt

PICTURE WINDOW
a capstone imprint

D1223788

My First Classic Story is published by Picture Window Books
A Capstone Imprint
1710 Roe Crest Drive
North Mankato, Minnesota 56003
www.capstonepub.com

Library of Congress Cataloging-in-Publication Data

Jones, Christianne C.
Beauty and the beast / retold by Christianne C. Jones
illustrated by Amy Bailey Muehlenhardt.
p. cm. — (My first classic story)
Summary: Through her great capacity to love, a kind
and beautiful maid releases a handsome prince from
the spell which has made him an ugly beast.
ISBN 978-1-4048-6081-0 (library binding)
ISBN 978-1-4795-1851-7 (paperback)
[1. Fairy tales. 2. Folklore—France.] I. Muehlenhardt, Amy
Bailey, 1974- ill. II. Beauty and the beast. English. III. Title.
PZ8.J535Be 2011
398.2—dc22
[E]   2010003104

Art Director: Kay Fraser
Graphic Designer: Emily Harris

The story of *Beauty and the Beast* has
been passed down for generations.
There are many versions of the story.
The following tale is a retelling of the
original version. While the story has
been cut for length and level, the basic
elements of the classic tale remain.

After the death of his wife, a rich merchant was left to raise his six children.

It was not an easy job. The older girls were jealous of their younger sister, Beauty.

During a storm at sea, the merchant lost his ships.

The family became poor. They moved into a small house in the country.

The boys worked in the field.

Beauty did all of the house chores. Her sisters did not help.

Weeks later, the merchant heard that one of his ships was spotted.

He went to find it.

The merchant found his ship, but it was empty. On his way home, he got lost. The merchant saw a large castle. He went for help, but no one was there.

He ate some food and stayed the night.

The next morning, the merchant picked a
rose for Beauty.

Suddenly, a large creature yelled, "Who steals a rose from me? I gave you food and a place to stay. You are very rude!"

"I'm sorry. I only wanted a rose for one of my daughters," said the merchant.

"To repay me, you must bring me one of your daughters," the Beast roared.

The merchant went to his family. He told
them what the Beast had said.

Beauty said she would go. Her father led
her to the Beast's castle.

At first, Beauty was scared of the Beast.
But soon they became good friends.

Each night, they ate supper together and shared stories.

One day, a man came to the castle. He told Beauty that her father was sick.

She went home and helped her father
get well.

Beauty's sisters said she couldn't leave
their father again or he would get sick.

Beauty missed the Beast, but she stayed with her family.

Everything was fine until she had a bad dream.

In her dream, the Beast was dying of a broken heart.

Beauty hurried back to the castle. She found the Beast lying on the grass.

"I love you!" cried Beauty.

With those words, the Beast turned into
a prince.

"Your kind heart broke the spell," he said.

Beauty's jealous sisters were turned into statues to guard the castle.

And Beauty and the prince married and lived a happy life.